RACHEL *to the* Rescue

Ellen Frances

Illustrated by Mark David

Supa Doopers

sundance

Copyright © 1997 Sundance Publishing

All rights reserved. No part of this publication may be reproduced, stored in a retrieval system or transmitted in any form or by any means, electronic, mechanical, photocopying, recording, or otherwise, without the prior written permission of the publisher.

For information regarding permission, write to:
Sundance Publishing
234 Taylor Street
Littleton, MA 01460

Published by
Sundance Publishing
234 Taylor Street
Littleton, MA 01460

Copyright © text Ellen Frances
Copyright © illustrations Mark David
Project commissioned and managed by
Lorraine Bambrough-Kelly, The Writer's Style
Cover and text design by Marta White

First published 1996 by
Addison Wesley Longman Australia Pty Limited
95 Coventry Street
South Melbourne 3205 Australia
Exclusive United States Distribution: Sundance Publishing

ISBN 0-7608-0772-8

PRINTED IN CANADA

Contents

1 Shocking

The tears in Rachel's eyes welled up threatening to spill onto her cheeks. It wasn't fair!

How could the city council do this? And what about the play they'd all been working on for so long?

The children who attended the After-School Program at St. Gregory's Church stared at the floor, sniffed, or wiped their noses on dirty sleeves as their leaders, Miss Banks and Mrs. McDonald, read the letter out loud.

t was from the council and it was bad news. The
ouncil was planning to tear down the old,
eglected church and replace it with a parking lot!

"The council people are only doing their job," Miss Banks explained.

The church is
adly in need of
epair and if the
uilding inspector says
t isn't safe then there's
othing we can do about it.

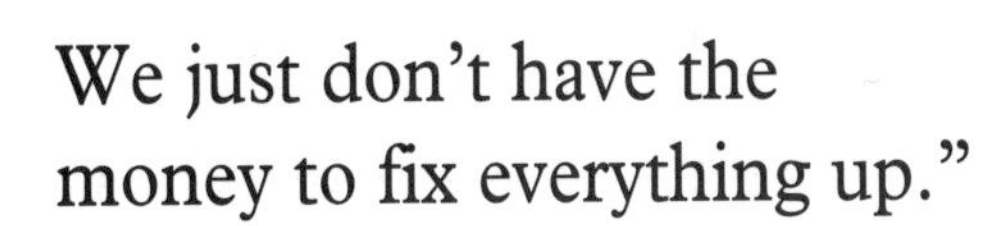

We just don't have the money to fix everything up."

She folded up the letter. “I’m sorry children, but you’ll have to find somewhere else to go from now on.” And with that, she hurried into her office.

Mrs. McDonald started clearing up the punch cups and fruit plates. "All right now," she said. "That's enough sulking. Your parents are waiting."
The children picked up their bags and silently shuffled outside.

Rachel didn't need to be picked up. She lived nearby, so close she could see the old church from her bedroom. On clear mornings, she liked to watch the stained-glass windows glittering in the sunlight.

She wandered sadly outside the building and climbed onto the oak tree near the back entrance. It was where she often went for comfort.

From its branches, she saw Miss Banks and Mrs. McDonald lock up and walk away, talking quietly.

"What are you doing up there?" demanded a crackly voice. Rachel nearly fell out of the tree. Mrs. Crabapple from next door had crept up on her.

"I'm not hurting anything," Rachel murmured. She was scared of Mrs. Crabapple — all the kids were. Mrs. Crabapple liked to yell at people and order them around.

"Didn't say you were doing anything," she hissed. "I asked what you were doing up there."

Rachel stared at her shoes. Mrs. Crabapple looked hard at her.

"You've been crying," she stated. "What have you got to cry about?"

"What do you care?" demanded Rachel.

She wanted the old woman to leave her alon

"None of your lip, girl," responded Mrs. Crabapple. "Just give me the story straight."

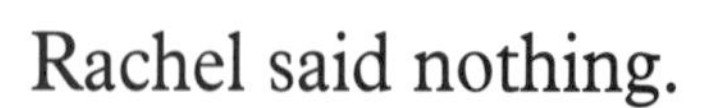

Rachel said nothing.

"You never know," Mrs. Crabapple muttered, "I might be able to help."

"Not a chance!" blurted out Rachel. But before she could stop herself, the whole story had burst out of her.

Mrs. Crabapple listened carefully, frowned, shook her head, and nodded. As Rachel ran out of words and breath, the old lady reached into a pocket and brought out a lace handkerchief.

"Here! Blow your nose," she instructed.

Rachel did as she was told and went to hand the hanky back.

"Don't be revolting, child!" hissed the old woman. "Give it a wash before you give it back."

"Now go home," Mrs. Crabapple ordered. "I've got some thinking to do."

Rachel jumped out of the tree and raced down to the church gate. When she turned around, Mrs. Crabapple had disappeared and only the wind was shuffling through the trees.

2

Never Say Die

The sounds of boxes being packed up greeted Rachel when she walked up the front steps of St. Gregory's the next day. She hoped they wouldn't ask her to help pack the place up. She'd only start crying again, and everyone would laugh at her!

She slipped out the back door and ran to the oak tree. Dropping her schoolbag, Rachel climbed onto its leafy branches. There was something stuck into a crevice between two twigs. It was a note on lavender paper! The words were in shaky, old-fashioned handwriting.

Never say die!

Tell your tale to someone who wants to know.

Underneath some pictures had been drawn.

Rachel stared at the pictures. They were a clue, but what did they mean? They reminded her of something — a game her class played where you had to count the number of lines on a Martian's face in order to solve a puzzle.

She started counting the petals on each flower. That was it! Count the petals on each flower, write these numbers together, and they make a phone number.

Rachel raced inside, slipped into the office while everyone was busy, and dialed the number she had just worked out.

"Piglington Gazette," a voice answered. "All the news and any news."

Lights, Camera, Action

The next afternoon, everyone at the After-School Program was excited. Rachel smiled to herself as Miss Banks combed her hair for the fifteenth time and Mrs. McDonald cleaned the sink for the twentieth.

"I can't believe it!" Miss Banks was saying. "How the *Piglington Gazette* found out about our problems, I'll never know!"

At that moment, there was a knock at the door. It was a reporter and photographer from the newspaper. Instantly, they were surrounded by the children. Miss Banks rescued the visitors and showed them around.

The photographer asked the 25 children to keep packing up the boxes. He took shot after shot of them.

"This is great!" he enthused. "Is there anything else you can show us?"

"What about our play?" suggested Rachel, who had crept up behind Miss Banks.

"Great idea!" shouted the reporter. "Let's see it!"

Rachel sneaked out to her tree while the others performed. She wasn't needed for this. She'd been the one who had painted the scenery and helped with the costumes: She wasn't a star! She hugged her secret to herself as she climbed back among the branches. This might save their church.

Then she saw it — another note stuck in the twigs. It read:

The battle's not won until it's done!

Then followed a jumbled sentence of letters and numbers.

2, 25 - 12, 1, 23. D, G, B, I, E. E. 13, 1, 25, S, N.

A = 1

Rachel looked at the last part again. Now it made sense. She pulled a pencil from her pocket and worked out the whole code.

That night, she asked her father to take her to the library. She searched through old council records until she found exactly what she was looking for.

Eggs in a Basket

The following afternoon after school, Rachel couldn't get to St. Gregory's quickly enough. In her hand was the information she'd collected the night before.

A crowd was gathered at the old church's door. The newspaper report had led some of the parents and neighbors to mount a protest against the closure. On the church steps stood the mayor, surrounded by a gaggle of TV cameras and reporters. Miss Banks and Mrs. McDonald were at one side, the children gathered around them.

"I've no idea who called you!" shouted the mayor. "It's not going to do them any good! We're a responsible council, and we wouldn't be doing our duty to the citizens of Piglington if we didn't make sure their children were safe and protected."

"But where are the children going to go now?" called out a reporter from the back of the pack.

"That's not our problem," answered the mayor. "I'm sure if people bothered to look they could find somewhere."

"Your protest isn't going to have any effect," he continued. "The decision has been made. Come Monday, this dump is coming down!" Storming down the steps, he climbed into a waiting police car and was whisked away.

A few of the children were crying as they moved inside with their leaders to finish packing up. Mrs. Crabapple hid behind her fence listening and scowling. She was the only one to see Rachel storm to the tree and hide in its branches. She waited until everyone had gone, then hobbled over.

"Still moping, are you?" she croaked.

"Of course not!" seethed Rachel. "It's just not fair."

"Life isn't fair!" Mrs. Crabapple threw back. "What's in your hand?"

"An old piece of paper!" Rachel spat out.

"Give it to me," ordered the old lady.

Without thinking, Rachel passed the paper down. Mrs. Crabapple was like that: She made people do things.

"I thought so," murmured Mrs. Crabapple as she read the sheet. "By-law 4 7 2 9 5. May 5, 1914."

She seemed to be remembering something. "Father was right. Old man Piglington, our city's founder, really is buried at the church."

Rachel stared at her. "You knew!" she gasped.

“Who do you think left the notes?” hissed the woman. “It was my father who built this church, and I’m not going to let them pull it down without a fight!” Mrs. Crabapple sighed. “Now get out of that tree. The show isn’t over until the fat lady sings.”

She shuffled home. Rachel slid out of the tree and followed her.

Treasure Map

Mrs. Crabapple's den was dark and musty.

"It's in here somewhere," the old lady wheezed, staring at the open cupboard in front of her.

"Let me do it," said Rachel as she knelt beside her. "What exactly are we looking for?"

"A large parcel, tied up in red ribbon with a gold seal on the outside," replied Mrs. Crabapple. "It contains my father's will and the plans to the church."

The old woman leaned on Rachel's shoulder as she stood up, then eased herself onto the sofa.

Rachel pushed cans and boxes aside and began to leaf through the papers inside the cupboard. Mrs. Crabapple chuckled to herself, "I've been meaning to get around to cleaning that cupboard out."

Rachel kept searching. Mrs. Crabapple dozed off. Just as Rachel thought there was nothing more to see except the wood at the back, her fingers closed around a solid wad of papers. She'd found what they were looking for.

Mrs. Crabapple lurched awake as Rachel scrambled to her feet. The old lady adjusted her glasses to read the faded words on the outside of the package.

"This is it," she whispered. "Well done, child. Go and make a cup of tea while I work out exactly what's here!"

Rachel found the kitchen, made a pot of tea, and placed some cookies on a plate. She carried them into the den.

“It’s all here,” said Mrs. Crabapple, rubbing her eyes tiredly. “But my father was a great one for a joke, and I can’t understand a word of what he’s written.”

Rachel looked over the old woman's shoulder. In her lap was the age-stained will. Most of it was in long words that Rachel couldn't understand, but at the end was a map. Rachel knew it was a treasure map — she had seen them in pirate books.

Mrs. Crabapple looked disappointed.

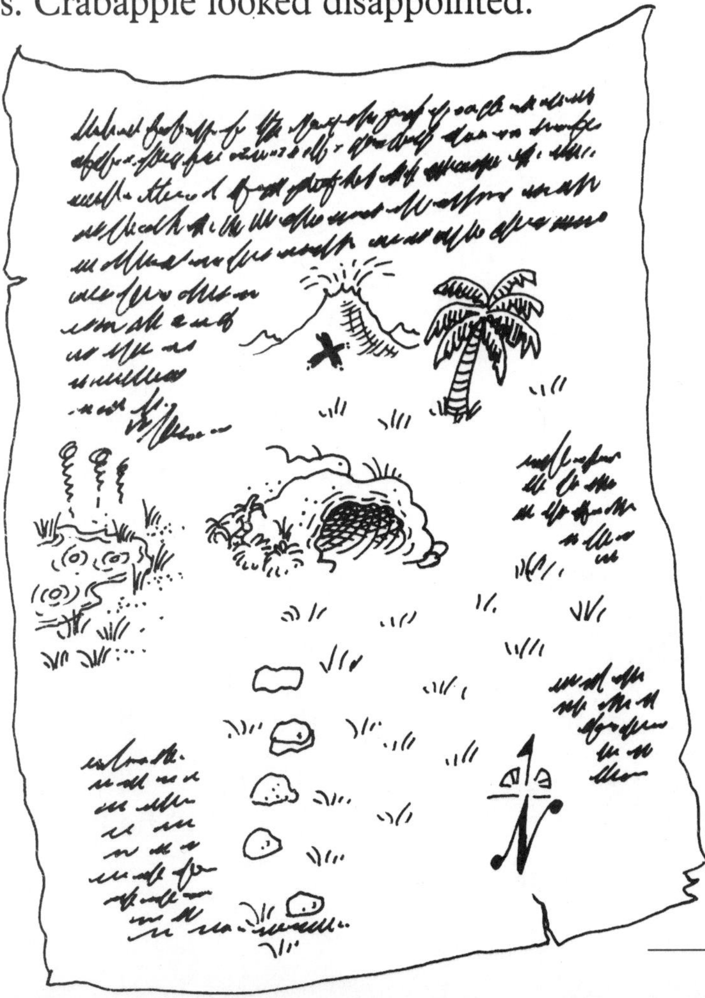

"Don't you worry," she told Mrs. Crabapple as she poured a cup of tea. "I'll work this puzzle out

"We haven't got long, dear," said Mrs. Crabapple in a weak voice. "The bulldozers will be here on Monday."

Rachel let herself out the front door.

"I've got to find out what the map's all about," she told herself firmly. "Everyone's depending on me even if they don't know it!" She hurried home to think.

Tracing Paper

The next day was Saturday. Rachel stayed inside all morning trying to work out the map. Just after lunch she went over to see Mrs. Crabapple. The old woman was lying on the sofa.

"I can't figure it out," Rachel told her. "I've looked at lots of treasure maps because I had to do a project about pirates for school. I used tracing paper to copy them onto my project sheet."

Mrs. Crabapple lifted her head a little. “What did you say?” she asked.

“My project sheet,” repeated Rachel. “I had to trace the maps onto my project sheet.”

“That’s it!” coughed Mrs. Crabapple and sat up. “The crafty old beggar,” she chuckled. “Pass me the map.”

Rachel placed the will in Mrs. Crabapple’s shaking hands. “Now the church plans,” she demanded.

Rachel sifted through the pile of papers in the cupboard until she found the right ones. Mrs. Crabapple pressed the map and the plans together and held them up to the light.

The two matched as if they were one! "Follow the map!" Mrs. Crabapple ordered Rachel. "Run to the church. I'll phone the mayor and Miss Banks. We'll meet you there. Hurry!"

Carrying the map and the plans, Rachel raced out of the house, through the gate, and up the path to the church steps.

She paused to hold the papers up to the sun. The rocks marked on the map covered the concrete steps shown on the plan! She counted them: There was the same number of rocks as there were steps. Mrs. Crabapple was right!

Rachel followed the paces drawn on the map. Twenty paces north. On the map, they ended at a palm tree. The old oak! Rachel ran to her hiding place.

Where to next? Ten paces southwest. That led her to the cave indicated on the map. The church's backdoor!

Fifteen paces west took her to the map's dark swamp. The church's smelly old outhouse!

Twelve paces east and another six north brought her up against the map's volcano. This was the church's back fence.

Here the trail ended, at a spot marked X. All Rachel could see was tall grass.

She tried to imagine what the area would have looked like when Mrs. Crabapple's father had drawn up the plans and built the church. She thought of the workmen, the smell of fresh paint, the young trees and the trampled, muddy earth where the garden surrounding the building would grow.

Of course! There would have been no grass here in those days.

Excitedly, Rachel started to stalk through the grass. Right up against a corner of the property she came to a crumbling gravestone.

Kneeling down she scraped away the dirt and moss hiding the words: J.R.G. PIGLINGTON. FIRST MAYOR OF PIGLINGTON. AN HONOR TO HAVE KNOWN HIM.

The Fat Lady Sings

Rachel heard voices. She looked up to see Miss Banks and the mayor helping Mrs. Crabapple through the tall grass.

"I don't believe it," said Miss Banks as she knelt to get a better look at the gravestone.

Mrs. Crabapple produced the council paper Rachel had found in the library.

"You can't pull the old church down now," she said to the mayor. "It's an important piece of our history and this Piglington City Council Bylaw of 1914 proves it! It declares this property a City Pride Monument, which should be cared for as long as this city is Piglington!"

The mayor sighed. "It seems we have been in error," he agreed, "but it still doesn't help you. The current council doesn't have the money to fix up the hall so we'll still have to shut down the After-School Program."

He looked at their disappointed faces. "I am really sorry," he said. "I wish there was some other way."

"If only we could raise some money," sighed Miss Banks.

Mrs. Crabapple nodded. "I'm afraid we're beaten this time," she said.

Rachel smiled. "No we're not," she corrected. "It's not over until the fat lady sings!" The two women stared at her.

"Let's put on the play and charge people money to see it!" she yelled.

The two women started to smile as well.

he next two days were a flurry of activity as veryone worked to unpack, clean up the church, nd get ready for the play. On Monday night, all f Piglington turned out to see what the children ad been doing. Even the mayor was there, itting in the front row and trying to make people elieve it was all his idea.

Rachel raced around with an enormous roll of tape, patching the holes in the backdrop and keeping the crepe-paper costumes hanging on the actors' backs. One by one, the acts went on to a great reception.

All too soon Mrs. McDonald was preparing to sing the national anthem in the final scene.

:veryone stood up. The mayor took off his hat
nd held it over his heart.

'Oh say, can you see, ..." Mrs. McDonald was a
ig woman with a powerful voice, and the little
hurch shook when she sang. Tears sprang to
eople's eyes, and a baby started to cry as she
eached the final line of the first verse. "And the
ome of the brave!" she boomed.

Then an amazing thing happened.

There was a cracking, shattering sound in the air. The stained-glass window behind the makeshift stage shattered into a thousand pieces!

Everyone gasped.
"What is that, glinting in the light, coming from the stage?"

Miss Banks stepped carefully through the glass and picked up a small, shiny box that had fallen down with the glass.

"It's money!" she whispered opening the lid.

"Lots of it! Our church is saved!"

Mrs. Crabapple hobbled over to Rachel standing behind the scenery. “The crafty old beggar,” she chuckled. “Dad made sure we’d get that money in the end.”

She looked down at the girl. "I told you it wasn'
over until the fat lady sang."

Rachel started to giggle and without thinking about what she was doing, gave Mrs. Crabapple a great big hug.